LYNN HUGGINS-COOPER grew up in Sussex and spent summer
afternoons tracing family history with her father. Childhood visits
to war cemeteries stimulated her interest in First World War history
and when she was researching Sydney's story, she traced his grave
in Belgium and visited it with her youngest daughter. Lynn has
degrees in law and Criminal Justice and has worked in a bail hostel,
as a teacher, a lecturer and a wildlife ranger at a lighthouse.
She has written over 200 books, mainly for children,
and now lives on an organic smallholding in County Durham
with her family.

IAN BENFOLD HAYWOOD studied Fine Art at the Nottingham
School of Art and Design and Illustration at the North Wales School
of Art and Design. He has been a community artist, a painter
and an art teacher. Ian has illustrated a number of children's books,
among them Linda Newbery's *Catcall,* which won a silver medal
in the Nestle Book prize, John Brindley's *The Rule of Claw*
and *The Usborne Book of Christmas Stories.*
He lives in Chester.

For Sydney Dobson, sent from Burnhope
in County Durham to fight and die on the fields of Belgium.
And for my dad, Dave Huggins, sent off to the Middle East
to do his military service. Unlike Sydney, Dad came home. – L.H.C

For all young men like Sydney – I.B.H.

One Boy's War copyright © Frances Lincoln Limited 2008
Text copyright © Lynn Huggins-Cooper 2008
Illustrations copyright © Ian P. Benfold Haywood 2008

The right of Lynn Huggins-Cooper to be identified as the Author of this work,
and of Ian P. Benfold Haywood to be identified as the Illustrator of this work,
has been asserted by them in accordance with the Copyright, Designs and Patents Act, 1988.

First published in Great Britain in 2008 and in the USA in 2009 by Frances Lincoln Children's Books,
4 Torriano Mews, Torriano Avenue, London NW5 2RZ
www.franceslincoln.com

First paperback published in Great Britain in 2010

A catalogue record for this book is available from the British Library.

ISBN: 978-1-84780-126-5

Printed in Dongguan, Guangdong, China by Toppan Leefung in July 2011

3 5 7 9 8 6 4 2

One Boy's War

Lynn Huggins-Cooper

Illustrated by Ian Benfold Haywood

F

FRANCES LINCOLN
CHILDREN'S BOOKS

WAR HAS BEEN DECLARED!

The papers are full of the news that the Germans have attacked France.

Pa is restless. His pals are rushing off in droves to join up. He says, "It's every man's duty to fight for King and Country." Ma scowls and clashes the pots together in the kitchen whenever he says that.

I wish I was older. I'll be sixteen just before Christmas. But Pa says the war will be over by then — hope not, not before I get a crack at the Kaiser!

PA'S GONE.
Last night, he crept into my room and told me he was going. He smelt faintly of tobacco and beer as he bent over me. His eyes were shining with excitement.

Ma didn't say a word this morning.
Her eyes were puffy and red-rimmed, though.
She grabbed my hand and hugged me close
as I left for work. I was glad none of the lads
could see. I'm not a bairn!

God, if only I was older!

I've made up my mind. I'm joining up.
Ma's smothering me.
From the moment I get in, her eyes are on me.

Everywhere I go I see flags and recruiting stations.
It's like they're calling to me. Pa always said
we should stand up against bullies – and what else
is the Kaiser, marching into France like that?

I'll lie about my age.
I'm tall, so there shouldn't be a problem.

I wonder where Pa is now?
I bet he'll be proud of me.

WELL, I MADE IT!

Bit sticky there for a moment. The recruiting sergeant eyed me up and down, and smirked when I said I was nineteen. But he took me anyway.

The training's been hard. I've put on lots of muscles, though! Don't dare write to Ma yet.

One lad told me he was sixteen. One of the other lads must have said something, because the next thing we knew, his mother turned up at the camp, full of hell!

Poor old Jim was 'claimed out', and the last we saw of him was his mother marching him down the road, boxing his ears as she went. I think Jim's ma could be a one-woman battalion – the Kaiser wouldn't stand a chance!

After that I kept quiet.

Poor Ma.

Hope she found the note I left.

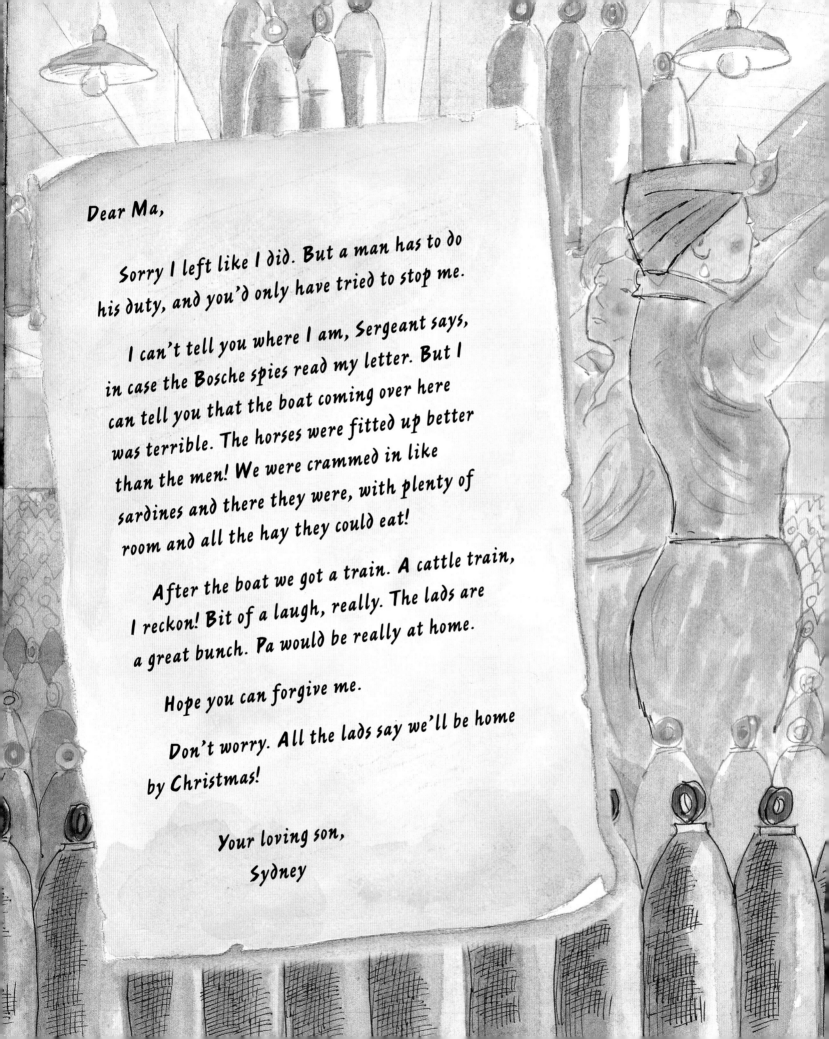

Dear Ma,

Sorry I left like I did. But a man has to do his duty, and you'd only have tried to stop me.

I can't tell you where I am, Sergeant says, in case the Bosche spies read my letter. But I can tell you that the boat coming over here was terrible. The horses were fitted up better than the men! We were crammed in like sardines and there they were, with plenty of room and all the hay they could eat!

After the boat we got a train. A cattle train, I reckon! Bit of a laugh, really. The lads are a great bunch. Pa would be really at home.

Hope you can forgive me.

Don't worry. All the lads say we'll be home by Christmas!

Your loving son,
Sydney

I never thought it would be like this.
When we started to dig the trenches, it still
seemed like a bit of a lark. Good hard work, a smoke, a laugh. Men's work.

But then the rain started. Torrents of it. The trenches are more like
muddy ponds. Yellow, soupy water soaks us as we trudge through
the muddy channels. I bet 'Wipers' was lovely once – green fields
and bird-filled hedges, just like Durham. Not now.

Then the fighting started.

One of the lads took a 'Blighty' today – off home with one leg gone below the knee, poor sod. Blown off by a shell. He's only nineteen. He'll never work again.

Beginning to wish it had been me.

It's the noise that gets to you. The pounding.
Like a thunderstorm that never ends. Then there's the weird
buzzing just over your head. Like angry bees, but with a far
deadlier sting. Bosche bullets, that's what they are.

Jonesy bought it today. One minute he was moaning about
the chloride of lime in the tea — said he wanted to drink it,
not bleach the latrines! Next minute, he was hunched over, coughing.
A horrible bubbling noise was choking up out of his chest.
All I could do was stare. He looked so scared. Then he went quiet.

I'd give anything to be back at home.

Dear Ma,

Don't believe all the scaremongering in
the papers. It's not too bad.

I had Bully Beef for tea again - with raw onions.
Not as good as your liver and bacon , but it'll do.
Loads of tea, and even plum and apple jam!

I haven't seen or heard anything about Pa.
Has he written?

I love you, Ma. Never forget that.

Anyway, Fritz is off again, so I'll close for now.
And don't forget - I'll be home by Christmas!

Your loving son,

Sydney

God help us if he's listening, which I doubt. I don't know what's worse –
the lice or the rats. My clothes are crawling and my skin is red-raw.
The itching's terrible. My mate Billy runs a match up the seams of
his khaki and you can hear the beggars pop – but there are always
more to take their place.

And the rats are so bold. They steal your food in broad daylight!
Last night Billy shot one – as big as a cat, I swear it was.
Wish I had Toff, my Pa's terrier. He'd show them a thing or two!

Hope Pa's better off than me.
Wonder where he is tonight.

I'm so sick of the wet. No matter how much
we bale the foul water out, it oozes straight back into
the trenches. We're soaked through all the time.
My feet are sore. "Trench Foot", the medic called it.
My feet stink. But all the lads are the same.

A shell hit nearby today. It was the strangest thing I've ever seen.
A wall of mud rose up where the shell hit, and surged towards us.
It broke over our heads like a wave, covering us in mud and stones.

I was talking to Billy when it hit. Our mouths filled with mud.
As I scrubbed my eyes, I caught sight of Billy's wide eyes staring
out of a face as black as the roads. I started laughing, but Billy
just carried on staring.

Poor old Billy. Such a comic. But he'll not be laughing again in this life.

Wish I was back home.

Well, we're waiting for "zero". At 08.45 hours
we'll be going over the top. The guns started pounding hours ago.
Pretty soon, we'll be up the ladders and over.

Please God, make me go. I don't want to let the lads down.
But I'm so scared. You feel so naked, running towards
those guns. Suppose the Bosche feel the same.

I hope there's not a bullet out there
with my name on it.

One of the lads has gone doolally —
crying, rocking, and calling for his ma
like a bairn. Can't blame him.

Every time I shut my eyes, I see myself doing that funny twirling dance you see when a lad goes down under fire.

Wish I was at home with my ma.

Soon, soon.
Won't be long, Ma.

My darling,

I'll be home soon. Injured at Ypres –
but don't worry your head, it's just
enough to send me home. It's been bad.
Really bad.
But it's over now – for me, anyway!
Tell Sydney I'll be home soon.
I've missed you both so much.
But knowing you both are safe
has kept me going.

Your Ever-loving Husband,

Peter

Sydney was a real young man. He was born in County Durham, but died in a muddy field in Belgium. His story is tragic. For millions of young men like Sydney there was no happy ending. Almost every family in Britain, Germany, France and Russia lost someone in the First World War.

At the beginning of the war, 'Pals' Battalions' went to fight together. These groups were made up of all the young men from a particular village or estate. Whole battalions were wiped out, leaving a village desolate, with no young men to return.

Many young boys lied about their age in order to join up. The youngest soldier to die was Private John Condon, who was only fourteen years old. But some soldiers were even younger. James Bartaby was only thirteen when he joined up, as was Myer Rosenblum from London.

Look around your town and see if you can find a war memorial. Read the names, and think about the poor young boys and men who died. Think of all the grieving families who lost them. Your old family photos may show men who fought – and even died – in World War I. Women died too. Many volunteered as nurses and ambulance drivers, living and dying in terrible conditions.

By the end of the First World War, 908,371 British men were dead and 2,090,212 came home wounded. Many men had to make new lives for themselves with terrible injuries and 'shell shock' – a form of mental illness brought on by the noise and horror of battle.

The First World War, or 'the Great War', as it was known, was supposed to be the War To End All Wars. Sadly, a second terrible war was to follow in 1939, and many more were to die.

Find out more about the real Sydney Dobson at www.oneboyswar.co.uk.

MORE TITLES FROM FRANCES LINCOLN CHILDREN'S BOOKS

TAIL-END CHARLIE
Mick Manning and Brita Granström

As a boy, Mick Manning listened to his father's hair-raising tales about life as an RAF airgunner during the Second World War. Now, years later, Mick has carefully recreated those stories, writing them down as if his dad was speaking the words. In collaboration with Brita, he has illustrated them too.

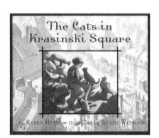

THE CATS IN KRASINSKI SQUARE
Karen Hesse
Illustrated by Wendy Watson

The cats in Krasinksi Square used to belong to someone. . .
And so did a little girl whose family has been destroyed by war. Even as she and her sister struggle to survive amid the war's chaos, they risk their lives on a plan to help those still trapped behind Warsaw's infamous Ghetto walls.

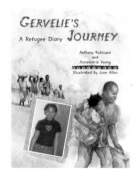

GERVELIE'S JOURNEY:
A Refugee Diary
Anthony Robinson and Annemarie Young
Illustrated by June Allan

When fighting broke out in Gervelie's home city of Brazzaville, her family had to flee to safety. Her father became a wanted man and was forced into hiding. The family was torn apart forever. Gervelie and her father escaped the country and travelled to the UK to seek asylum.
Anthony Robison and Annemarie Young relate this true story through Gervelie's words.